DINOSAUR TREE

by Douglas Henderson

Bradbury Press New York

Maxwell Macmillan Canada • Toronto
Maxwell Macmillan International
New York • Oxford • Singapore • Sydney

The accuracy of the facts and their interpretation are entirely the responsibility of the author. I wish to thank Robert A. Long for sharing with me over the years much information from his personal Triassic library. I wish to thank Vince Santucci for our discussions about the Triassic trees. And I wish to thank Patricia Lauber and Dr. Donald Baird for their comments.

Bradbury Press
Macmillan Publishing Company
866 Third Avenue
New York, NY 10022

Maxwell Macmillan Canada, Inc.
1200 Eglinton Avenue East
Suite 200
Don Mills, Ontario M3C 3N1

Macmillan Publishing Company is part of the Maxwell Communication Group of Companies.

First edition
Printed in Singapore

10 9 8 7 6 5 4 3 2 1

The text of this book is set in Aster.
Typography by Julie Y. Quan

The title page shows a petrified log in
Petrified Forest National Park in Arizona;
the dedication page depicts a wood-boring beetle
from the late Triassic.

LIBRARY OF CONGRESS CATALOGING-IN-PUBLICATION DATA
Henderson, Douglas.
Dinosaur tree / by Douglas Henderson.—1st ed.
p.   cm.
Includes index.
ISBN 0-02-743547-4
1. Trees, Fossil—Juvenile literature.   2. Dinosaurs—Juvenile
literature [1. Plants, Fossil.   2. Dinosaurs.] I. Title.
QE991.H46 1994
560'.1762—dc20   93-34204

To the Gardiner gang on the Yellowstone,
who told me to go outside and draw

CONTENTS

Introduction · 6

225 Million Years Ago · 9

Four Years Have Passed · 10

Fifty Years Have Passed · 13

The Tree Is 200 Years Old · 14

The Tree Is 300 Years Old · 16

400 Years Have Passed · 19

The Tree Has Grown for 500 Years · 20

Several Months Pass · 23

Day Turns to Evening · 24

A Day Passes · 27

Another Day Passes · 28

A Year Passes, Then Many More · 31

Glossary/Index · 32

INTRODUCTION

Some years ago I visited Petrified Forest National Park, which is located some thirty miles east of Holbrook, Arizona. The park is well known for the abundance of fossil logs that lie scattered across its Painted Desert landscape. During the late Triassic, some 225 million years ago, these fossil logs were living conifers, or cone-bearing trees. They grew as forests in a warm, humid region close to the equator and near the western margin of the large Triassic continent called Pangaea. Traces of these forests can be found today in Arizona, Utah, New Mexico, and Texas.

Diverse groups of ancient reptiles, both large and small, lived in these forests, including some of the first dinosaurs.

6

Hoping to decide what the old trees looked like, I walked through many of the park's fossil-log areas. All about were finely preserved stone trunks and stumps resting where a Triassic river had left them long ago. I could clearly see the fluted pattern of wood surfaces, the buttressed bases of trunks, traces of great roots, and the holes and swollen scars where large limbs had once been attached. Many of their features resembled those of Monterey cypress, an ancient conifer that grows today on the coast of California.

I was also reminded of trees I've seen during summers spent hiking in the Sierra Nevada, through forests of pine, cedar, fir, and juniper. I've crossed streams over their fallen trunks and slept exhausted under their high limbs. The blending of quiet and light and stillness across halls of huge trees, all punctuated by small, singing birds, was a gift from the sequoia groves I wandered through and that I remember still.

I have always wanted to include these experiences, that rich sense of place, in my illustrations of ancient plants and animals. This story's pastel paintings of old Triassic trees are based on my observations of the fossil logs, library research, guesswork, and my impressions of living conifers. I imagine that the old trees lived in a world as bright and beautiful as our own.

Douglas Henderson
Whitehall, Montana

225 MILLION YEARS AGO

It is a time when dinosaurs live in the Triassic forest. Above the banks of a stream, a great conifer tree is shedding seeds from the small cones on its branches. One seed drifts down through the air. It falls to the forest floor and tumbles into the damp soil. After a time, warmed by the sun, the tree seed begins to sprout. Slowly, a root grows straight down into the soil and a shoot of small leaves grows up toward the light. Days go by. When the leaves rise above the ground, they shine green in their first days of sunlight.

The tree is tiny, weighing less than an ounce. Just above the little tree are the bigger leaves of ferns that grow across the forest floor. Though the tree is small, already its roots gather water and its leaves take in the air and soak up the sunlight. Each day the tree grows a little bigger.

FOUR YEARS HAVE PASSED

The little tree has grown taller than the low ferns. Now it is several feet high, with small, needle-like leaves on the ends of its branches. Just above grow taller plants, like cycads and tree ferns. The little tree grows straight up, its branches spreading wider to reach more light.

The tree needs light. Like all green plants, the tree makes its own food. Within its leaves it combines nutrients from the air and soil with sunlight. This makes sugars, which the tree feeds on to grow. As it grows, the tree also gives off water and oxygen. Oxygen is what the animals in the forest need to breathe.

When the tree makes food for itself, it is also making food for the forest animals. The tree becomes food for plant-eating animals. In turn, the plant-eating animals are food for the meat-eating animals.

The tree is in danger of being eaten because many plant-eating reptiles roam the stream banks and the quiet, shadowed forest. Once, a small dinosaur, a *Revueltosaurus,* stopped and looked right at the little tree, then walked on. The little tree just kept growing, slowly turning air and sunlight into more leaves and roots and wood.

FIFTY YEARS HAVE PASSED

The tree has grown taller than the highest cycads and tree ferns. It has entered the great open space between the ground and the lower limbs of the older, taller conifer trees. The tree's upper branches reach sixty feet in the air, a place filled with light. Here, each morning, from the sun-warmed tops of the old trees, comes the quiet hum of millions of insects.

Herds of *Placeria*, large, plant-eating dicynodonts, wander below the tree. They are mammal-like reptiles with tusks and big, turtle-like beaks. But they cannot reach the high branches of the young tree.

THE TREE IS 200 YEARS OLD

Now the tree spreads a cool shade on the forest floor. The tree weighs many tons, but its ever-growing roots anchor it in the ground. The tree is tall, and its limbs reach far out over the stream below. Leaves hang from its branches like green clouds.

Within the tree's branches are open spaces, like rooms, where creatures flutter between light and shade. Some are flying insects. Some are gliding, lizard-like reptiles. Some are pterosaurs.

Around the tree the forest keeps changing. In the quiet days and nights, a sudden great crash means another old tree has fallen.

There are times in the year when it rains day after day. Thunder rolls over the forest, and the stream beneath the tree fills with swift, roaring water. Other times there are long dry spells. The air becomes hot and dusty, and the stream may dry up. But throughout the year, each day warms the resin within the bark and wood of the conifer trees. Then a scent like pine, juniper, and cedar fills the forest.

THE TREE IS 300 YEARS OLD

After so many peaceful years, the Earth beneath the tree has begun to tremble. There are sounds of distant explosions. A cloud of steam and volcanic ash rises from a far-off mountain. A volcano is erupting. White, dusty ash falls from the sky day and night. It coats the forest white and turns the stream to flowing mud. The ash flattens the ferns on the forest floor and weighs down the limbs of the tall trees.

The ash blocks the sun and the daylight grows dim. From across the forest, there comes the crashing sound of breaking tree limbs falling to the forest floor. Then all becomes quiet. The eruption ends. When the rains come again, they wash the forest clean.

The tree has lost some of its limbs because of the heavy volcanic ash. But the ash has added minerals to the soil. Below the tree the ferns grow back. Slowly, they cover the tree's fallen limbs, which are scattered about its buttressed trunk. The tree grows larger.

400 YEARS HAVE PASSED

A great tree stands where once a seed started to grow. The tree is nearly two hundred feet high, and its trunk is ten feet thick. Tons of leaves hang from its big limbs. Over its long life, the tree's leaves have given off large amounts of oxygen into the air. They have also released millions of gallons of water into the air, water taken up by the tree's roots—water that formed into clouds and fell as rain far away. The tree has helped to make a world where other plants and animals can live.

A small reptile moves among the shadows and sandstone boulders of the stream bank. It is *Hesperosuchus*, a meat-eating, fleet-footed sphenosuchid. Passing beneath the old tree, it searches for insects and smaller reptiles to eat.

Time is beginning to weaken the tree. Some of its roots are dead, and more are rotting from the growth of fungi. Wood-boring grubs and beetles tunnel under the tree's bark, causing limbs and leaves to die. The tree weighs one hundred tons and now is starting to lean out over the stream. But the tree captures sunlight each morning and grows still bigger.

THE TREE HAS GROWN
FOR 500 YEARS

One day a rising wind blows through the forest. It whistles in the branches of the old tree. In the past strong winds buffeted the tree, yet it stood in its place. But now the wood of its roots is weak from decay. When the wind pushes harder on the leaves and trunk, the tree moves. Slowly, it begins to fall, and then it gathers speed. With the sound of its roots tearing apart, the tree rushes toward the ground. It hits with a thundering crash. Then all is quiet.

The tree lies across the streambed, its top broken off. Most of its limbs are broken off, too. The stream flows quietly under and around the fallen tree.

The life of the old tree has ended. But many of its seeds, carried off by the wind over the years, have grown into trees throughout the forest.

A large cynodont, a meat-eating, mammal-like reptile looking something like a dog, wanders near the broken tree.

SEVERAL MONTHS PASS

The old tree rests across the stream like a bridge. Scattered about are the tree's broken limbs and mats of leaves slowly turning brown in the warm sun. Two *Chindeosaurus*, small meat-eating dinosaurs, travel across the fallen tree at night in the moonlight.

Then the wet season begins. It rains for days. The stream fills with water and becomes a roaring flood. The water spills around and over the fallen tree. The tree begins to move and to plow through the gravel. It swings downstream like a weather vane in a wind. The water lifts the tree and carries it along in its strong current.

Now the tree is racing through the forest, traveling the course of the wild stream. It passes a *Trilophosaurus*, a lizard-like reptile.

23

DAY TURNS TO EVENING

The stream plunges down through the hills. The flooding water knocks the tree against the channel bottom and against other old trees caught in the current. The last of the tree's limbs are torn away. All of its bark is scraped off, and its big roots are worn to stubs. The tree is now a smooth, slippery, wet log.

The stream sweeps out of the low mountains and into a broad, forested plain, taking the tree with it. Growing less turbulent, the stream joins with other streams to form a large, muddy river which flows on for many miles.

The flooded river carries the tree past riverbanks piled with old logs left by earlier floods. At one place on the bank, large reptiles move in the twilight. A meat-eating thecodont, *Postosuchus*, preys on a plant-eating, armored thecodont called *Desmatosuchus*. The old tree flows on.

A DAY PASSES

The old tree slows as it reaches a calm bend in the river. The muddy waters are beginning to clear. Swimming below the tree are many fish. One is *Chinlea,* a freshwater coelacanth. Some are sleek freshwater sharks. Large, stubby-legged amphibians called metoposaurs swim in the river, hunting for fish and small aquatic reptiles.

The tree floats past stream banks, where large horsetails and other small shore plants grow. In places, the forest of tall trees grows right to the river's edge. Whole trees have fallen into the water where the river washed under their roots.

Large reptiles swim past the tree. They are phytosaurs, long-snouted, fish-eating thecodonts, looking much like crocodiles. Rows of phytosaurs line the shore in places, basking in the sun.

ANOTHER DAY PASSES

The tree is carried by the river into a changing land. The river begins to meander, flowing in wide curves across the level plain. The forest becomes thinner, with clumps of trees divided by wide mudflats.

Ahead of the tree, a herd of large dinosaurs fords the river. They are prosauropods, animals that walk on four legs, with long necks and tails. In the deeper water, only their necks rise above the smooth, flowing current. When they cross a sandbar in the river, each animal climbs onto the low, wet island, then plunges back into the water, heading for shore.

The river carries the tree toward the sandbar. Here, the water grows shallow and the current weakens. The tree's buttressed trunk drags on the river bottom. On the edge of the sandbar, the tree comes to a stop. All around are other logs left here by the river. They cause ripples in the shallow water that flows around them. When the flooding is over, the river water lowers. The sandbar and all the old logs on it are left drying in the sun.

A YEAR PASSES,
THEN MANY MORE

The old tree is slowly decaying in the rain and warm sun. Ferns carpet the island. Animals like *Coelophysis,* a small meat-eating dinosaur, pass by from time to time. Then there is another flood. The river rises. It washes over the tree and quickly covers it with mud and silt. More floods follow. Over centuries the river buries the log far below the surface.

Slowly, the log becomes a fossil. Bit by bit its wood is replaced by tiny grains of silica from volcanic ash in the mud that surrounds the tree. Eventually, the tree is no longer made of wood. It has become a fossil log made of stone. A very long time passes, a time from then to now. Life on the Earth has changed. The Triassic forest has long ago vanished. All of its species of plants and animals, including all of the dinosaurs, have become extinct.

Today, in the Painted Desert in Arizona, all that remains of the old Triassic forest are fossil bones and leaves and great stone logs resting on the ground.

GLOSSARY/INDEX

AMPHIBIANS   Cold-blooded animals with backbones that must return to water to lay their eggs. Many amphibians are aquatic. **27**

BUTTRESSED TRUNK   The broad swelling at the base of a tree's trunk that supports the tree's increasing weight. **7, 16, 28**

CEDAR   A modern group of conifers. **7, 14**

CHINDEOSAURUS   A small, meat-eating dinosaur related to the first dinosaurs to appear in the fossil record. *Chindeosaurus* was first discovered in Petrified Forest National Park. **23**

CHINLEA   A five-foot-long coelacanth that lived during the Triassic in streams and lakes in the southwestern United States. **27**

COELACANTHS   A group of lobe-finned fish that first appear in the fossil record during the Middle Devonian some 380 million years ago. They lived in both freshwater and marine environments during the Triassic. One species lives today in the Indian Ocean. **27**

COELOPHYSIS   A ten-foot-long, fifty-pound, meat-eating dinosaur that lived throughout North America during the Triassic. **31**

CONES   A reproductive structure formed by modified leaves in which seeds develop. **6, 9**

CONIFER   A cone-bearing tree. Conifers have lived on Earth for 300 million years. **6, 7, 9, 13, 14**

CYCADS   Palm-like plants with a radial cluster of tough leaves atop a thick, slow-growing stem. Cycads reproduce from cones. **10, 13**

CYNODONTS   A group of both plant-eating and meat-eating mammal-like reptiles that developed many anatomical features of mammals. **20**

DESMATOSUCHUS   A fifteen-foot-long aetosaur. Aetosaurs were armor-plated, plant-eating thecodonts. **24**

DICYNODONTS   A group of stout, plant-eating, mammal-like reptiles with turtle-like beaks, shearing jaws, and heavy limbs. **13**

DINOSAURS   A group of advanced reptiles that flourished during the Mesozoic Era. **6, 9, 10, 23, 28, 31**

FERNS   Seedless vascular plants with delicate leaves, or fronds, that reproduce by spores and spreading, underground stems. **9, 10, 16, 31**

FOSSIL   Any object, cast, or impression that shows evidence of ancient life. **6, 7, 31**

FUNGI   Plant-like organisms that feed on and cause the decomposition of organic matter. **19**

GREEN PLANTS   Plants that make their own food by combining minerals and water from the soil with carbon dioxide from the air, using energy from sunlight to manufacture sugars. **10**

HESPEROSUCHUS   A five-foot-long, meat-eating reptile related to crocodiles. **19**

JUNIPER   A modern conifer. **7, 14**

MAMMAL-LIKE REPTILES   A diverse group of animals called therapsids that developed many anatomical features of mammals on an ancestral reptilian frame. Modern mammals are thought to have developed from the therapsids. **13, 20**

METOPOSAURS A group of large, flat-headed amphibians that lived in the streams and lakes of the southwestern United States during the Triassic. Some metoposaurs reached ten feet in length. **27**

PAINTED DESERT A region in the southwestern United States comprised of brightly colored mud and sandstones deposited by streams and rivers during the Triassic. **6, 31**

PANGAEA A single, large continent that existed during the Triassic in which all the Earth's landmass was joined. **6**

PHYTOSAURS A group of meat-eating reptiles that resembled, but were not related to, crocodiles. Phytosaurs were thecodonts. Many different species of phytosaurs lived in and along the streams of the southwestern United States during the Triassic. Some phytosaurs reached thirty feet in length. **27**

PINE A modern group of conifers. **7, 14**

PLACERIA A ten-foot-long dicynodont that lived in the southwestern United States during the Triassic. **13**

POSTOSUCHUS A fifteen-foot-long rauisuchian. Rauisuchians were a group of meat-eating thecodonts that walked on four legs. The rauisuchians developed hind limbs held more under the body, allowing them to carry their weight more efficiently. **24**

PROSAUROPODS A group of large, plant-eating dinosaurs that walked on four legs and developed small heads and long necks and tails. **28**

PTEROSAURS A group of reptiles that flew with wings comprised of a membrane that extended between a long single finger bone on each hand and its body. **14**

REPTILES Cold-blooded animals with backbones and having skin covered with scales or plates of armor. Most reptiles reproduce by laying eggs. **6, 10, 14, 19, 20, 23, 24, 27**

REVUELTOSAURUS A small, plant-eating dinosaur that walked on two legs. *Revueltosaurus* is known from teeth found in Petrified Forest National Park. **10**

SILICA Silicon dioxide, a white, powdered quartz or glass. **31**

SPECIES A kind or type of living thing. **31**

SPHENOSUCHIDS A group of small reptiles related to modern crocodiles. **19**

SUGAR A food product that is manufactured by plants using sunlight and that stores some of the energy in sunlight. Some sugars are used by plants as food, and other sugars are manufactured to be used as building blocks for various plant structures. **10**

THECODONTS A diverse group of advanced reptiles that lived during the Triassic. Dinosaurs are thought to have developed from the thecodonts. Thecodonts became extinct after the early Mesozoic. **24, 27**

TREE FERN A plant related to ferns, with a cluster of long fronds atop a tall vascular column, or heavy stem. **10, 13**

TRIASSIC A span of time making up the first period of the Mesozoic Era, from 245 million years to 208 million years ago. **6, 7, 9, 31**

TRILOPHOSAURUS A ten-foot-long, lizard-like, plant-eating reptile with a beak like a turtle's and powerful digging claws. *Trilophosaurus* lived across the southwestern United States during the Triassic. **23**

VOLCANIC ASH Very fine grains of glass or silica ejected from the vent of a volcano. **16, 31**